For Alan and Amanda —J.W. xx

American edition published in 2018 by Andersen Press USA,
an imprint of Andersen Press Ltd.
www.andersenpressusa.com

First published in Great Britain in 2017 by Andersen Press Ltd.,
20 Vauxhall Bridge Road, London SW1V 2SA.

Text copyright © Jeanne Willis, 2017.
Illustration copyright © Tony Ross, 2017.

Distributed in the United States and Canada by
Lerner Publishing Group, Inc.
241 First Avenue North
Minneapolis, MN 55401 USA
For reading levels and more information, look up this title at www.lernerbooks.com.

Printed and bound in Malaysia.

Library of Congress Cataloging-in-Publication Data Available
ISBN: 978-1-5415-1456-0
eBook ISBN: 978-1-5415-1473-7
1—TWP—8/1/17

The T-Rex who Lost his Specs!

Jeanne Willis

Tony Ross

ANDERSEN PRESS USA

There was a T-Rex who lost his specs
and got himself in trouble.

Everything seemed very blurred
and sometimes he saw . . .

He did not recognize his clothes
when he was getting dressed . . .

... so put his sister's undies on
and wore his granny's vest.

He went to give himself a wash,
but could not find the basin . . .

. . . and so the toilet was the place
that T-Rex washed his face in.

Then when he went to dry himself,
he thought he'd grabbed a towel . . .

... but rubbed himself all over
with a prehistoric owl.

He went to make his breakfast,
but believing they were kippers . . .

. . . he fried and ate his brother's sock
and toasted Grandpa's slippers.

And, as it was a windy day,
he went to fetch his kite.

But since he could not find the string,
he tied a new one—tight.

Although the kite put up a fight,
he dragged it through the door,
not realizing that it was . . .

Convinced its cries were just the wind,
the T-Rex climbed the hill . . .

... in fact it was a brontosaurus
lying very still!

The "hill" stood up! The "kite" took off!
What happened to T-Rex?

Some like to think he is extinct
because he lost his specs.

In truth, his best friends saved him—
they were such a friendly bunch.
They helped him find his glasses, but . . .

. . . he dropped them in his lunch.
He ate them by mistake, and having lost his specs once more,
he ran to Mommy but he hugged . . .

. . . the wrong mom dinosaur!